S0-AIY-048

for Suren,
who was so deeply and utterly loved
by his mama, aunty, aachchi, seeya, and family

• • •

සදාතනික සුවඳක්, අපරිමිත සෙනෙහසක් අප හද තුල ජනිත කල සුරේන් පුතුට,
ආදර අම්මා, පුංචි අම්මා, ආච්චි, සීයා සහ පවුලේ සැම

Published by Roaring Brook Press
Roaring Brook Press is a division of Holtzbrinck Publishing Holdings Limited Partnership
120 Broadway, New York, NY 10271 • mackids.com

Copyright © 2023 by Dinalie Dabarera
All rights reserved.

Library of Congress Control Number: 2022910331
ISBN 978-1-250-82427-1

Our books may be purchased in bulk for promotional, educational, or business use.
Please contact your local bookseller or the Macmillan Corporate and Premium Sales Department
at (800) 221-7945 ext. 5442 or by email at MacmillanSpecialMarkets@macmillan.com.

First edition, 2023
The illustrations in this book were created with colored pencil on paper. This book was edited by Connie Hsu,
with art direction and design by Aram Kim. The production editor was Mia Moran,
and the production was managed by Jie Yang. The type was set in Eurocrat.

Printed in China by RR Donnelley Asia Printing Solutions Ltd., Dongguan City, Guangdong Province

1 3 5 7 9 10 8 6 4 2

Quiet Time with My Seeya

DINALIE DABARERA

Roaring Brook Press

New York

Time with my seeya is quiet time.

CHOO

Mostly.

Mum says that's because Seeya and I
speak different languages.

But that doesn't matter to us,
because my seeya and I like
all the same things.

We like playing
dress-up.

And stomping
in puddles.

Finding bugs in
the yard.

Just not spiders!

I like helping my
seeya in the garden.

I water the flowers.

Seeya waters
the pots.

Seeya likes
helping me
beat the
baddies.

He's not very good.

But he tries his best.

Sometimes, my seeya reads to me.
I don't know all the words,

but I get what he means.

We love playing "show-and-tell."

We show a lot more than we tell.

"Balla balla,"

says Seeya, laughing.

"Dog dog!"

We howl.

"Yum!"

I say as we
make pittu.

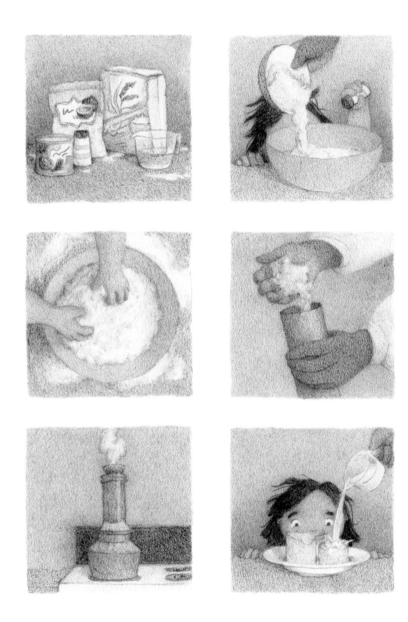

"Aiyoo," teases Seeya
when I'm messy.

Seeya is much worse.

Seeya and I go on all kinds
of adventures together.

We

zip!

And

we

sizzle.

We splash!

And we sparkle.

Sometimes,
it's my turn to
read to Seeya.

He doesn't know all the words,
but I can tell . . .

. . . he knows what I mean.

AUTHOR'S NOTE

The last time I visited my grandma in her nursing home, she beckoned me over to sit by her side, as she always did. She took my hand in both of hers and held it, patting, gently stroking, telling me without words that she was happy to see me.

Love is a word I'm lucky to understand in Sinhalese, the language of my grandmother. *Godak aadharei* means "to love very much." As I got older, Sinhalese became less a part of my daily life. Communicating with my grandma grew increasingly more difficult, coincidentally as my desire to know her better grew, too.

When my grandmother migrated to Australia to be with her daughters and their children, she left behind the only life she'd ever known: her home, her family and friends, her culture, and her language. She loved being around people, but in Australia most of her outside social interactions were limited to a smile. Her world must have gotten very small.

Growing up among the children of immigrants, I had friends who didn't speak any of the same languages as their grandparents, and yet had such a close and affectionate bond that remains to this day. That's not to say it's never hard; when you're trying to love across languages and cultures, missteps and misunderstandings abound. Distance can grow.

Even so, when I think of my grandma and her hands holding mine, soft and crinkly and warm, I know her love for me was bigger than all of that.

This is a book about that love—the kind of love that is communicated in time and attention, in play and laughter, and in being together.

ON MY GRANDMA'S LAP, WITH MY SISTER, BACK IN THE OLD COUNTRY (SRI LANKA, SOMETIME DURING THE '80S).